Disney's

TREASURE PLANET

JIM'S JOURNAL

As told to Eduardo Vitamina

Illustrated by
Andy Gaskill
Art Director of
Disney's Animated Feature
Treasure Planet

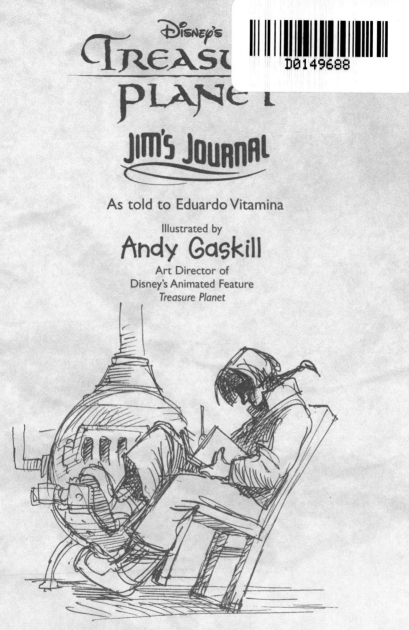

Designed by Disney's Global Design Group

A STEPPING STONE BOOK™

Random House 🏠 New York

Copyright © 2002 Disney Enterprises, Inc. All rights reserved under International
and Pan-American Copyright Conventions. Published in the United States by
Random House Children's Books, a division of Random House, Inc., New York,
and simultaneously in Canada by Random House of Canada Limited, Toronto,
in conjunction with Disney Enterprises, Inc. RANDOM HOUSE and colophon are regis-
tered trademarks and A STEPPING STONE BOOK and colophon are
trademarks of Random House, Inc.

Library of Congress Control Number: 2001097102

ISBN: 0-7364-2018-5

Printed in the United States of America

10 9 8 7 6 5 4 3 2

www.randomhouse.com/kids/disney

Yeah! Had the best solar surfing day ever! I couldn't believe it. I was down by the old quarry on my solar surfer when guess who showed up? Ray Quandree, the best solar surfer ever to ride the winds on Montressor. And that old solar dog challenged me—yeah, me—to a race!

RAY

I figured what the heck, nothing to lose, right? So I kicked my surfer into gear. I had no idea whether that new crystal capacitor I had installed yesterday was gonna work. Would it zip me into a fast lead—or a fast nosedive if I stalled out?

But it only took a few seconds to see that it was working. Boy, was it working! I've never cruised so fast in my life. I left Ray in the solar dust. He was so far behind, I couldn't even see him!

But not for long. Next thing I knew, he was clipping out of some shortcut he had found in an old mine shaft. I guess if you're gonna be the best at this game, you have to have some tricks up your sleeve.

I had to catch him, so I pushed the capacitor into high gear. My surfer shot into the lead again! Then suddenly we were at the finish. I won by a nose!

Ray was pretty cool, but he didn't like losing. He wants me to meet him again soon for another race. Fine with me. I would solar surf all day if Mom let me.

Speaking of Mom, I better finish this up and get going. Time to bus the tables at the Benbow Inn. I wonder if that little Loppytonian, Angela Legintoe, will spill her Zirellian jellyworms all over the table again.

Gross!

Oh, well. It's okay. I know Mom needs me. Someday I'm going to find a way to help her so she won't have to work so hard. Till then, it's bus the tables and wash the dishes.

Benbow Inn's #1 dishwasher

SOLAR SURFING

Tacking: Turning your surfer 180 degrees toward the sun. Balance and steering are important when tacking.

Gybing: Turning your surfer 180 degrees away from the sun. Again, balance and steering are important.

Carving: Turning the board on its edge and "carving" it through the etherium. It's amazing, but it takes lots of practice.

Chop hopping: "Getting air" from a solar swell. Conditions have to be just right—too much crosswind and you'll totally wipe out!

Cygnus spin: The ultimate trick—for experts only. It's a combination of a carve, a gybe, and a 360-degree spin. If you want to get really fancy, try it with no hands!

Remember!

Balance: Always keep your knees slightly bent. Keep your weight on the balls of your feet. Try to keep your feet in the middle of the board at all times.

Steering: Lean forward or backward, depending on the strength of the sun. Use the direction of the sail to your advantage.

Date: 01.0–062.50
Place: Montressor

Man, Montressor can be a small planet sometimes. There's nothing to do here.

Today an old spacer staying at the Benbow said he thinks he remembers shipping out with my dad once. They were going to save an Orcus galacticus from a spacer's net. Sweet! I'd love to do that.

But when he started asking about my dad, I told him I had to bus some more tables. I wanted him to tell me stuff about my dad, but I didn't want to have to talk about him. . . . He's gone—and talk won't bring him back.

One cool thing happened today. I got the Cygnus spin just right. I've been trying to pull off that trick on the surfer since the last lunar eclipse. Too bad Ray Quandree wasn't around to see me!

When I got home, Mom had a ton of chores for me to do. Like cleaning the bullyadous's stall, clearing tables, even fixing one of the service robots. I was pretty tired, and I accidentally dropped a whole tray of dishes.

Mom was upset, I could tell. "Jim, we can't afford . . . ," she started to say—and then she stopped. She knew I felt terrible. I'm gonna try and glue some of the dishes together tonight after she goes to bed.

Mom

Date: 01.0—077.00
Place: Montressor

Tonight at dinner, I overheard two Calyan spacers telling stories about the treasure of Captain Nathaniel Flint. I loved reading those stories when I was a little kid.

Flint was the most ruthless pirate around. He would launch surprise attacks on merchant ships in every corner of the universe. And then, as suddenly as he appeared, he would disappear. He got away with tons of gold, gems, and Arcturian solar crystals.

No one knows how he did it. No spacer in the etherium was safe.

Even the queen's entire armada couldn't stop him.

They say Flint hid the booty far beyond the Magellanic Cloud. Maybe somewhere in the Coral Galaxy.

Somewhere out there is a place called Treasure Planet that holds the loot of a thousand worlds! Nobody knows exactly where it is. But supposedly there is a map. . . .

If I had that map, I would find Treasure Planet in a second!

Date: 02.0–065.00
Place: Montressor

At dinner tonight, one of the Xenusian guests at the inn saw me writing in this journal. He patted me on the back and said, "Good work, son. All real spacers keep a journal of their adventures."

I told him life on Montressor isn't exactly an adventure.

He laughed and said, "Someday you'll get your chance, young brigand." I sure hope so....

Today the robot cops almost nabbed me. But I'm way too quick for them. I was surfing down by the old quarry again. No one's allowed down there. But it's the best place to ride.

I've been thinking more about Flint's treasure. What would I do with a pirate's bounty? I'd build the fastest and coolest solar surfer around. It would have Saturnian sails, a turbocharged ether capacitor, a brand-new pair of galactorails, and a board made of PURE VICTORIUM!

With that kind of surfer, I'd be able to win all the big races, even the Galactic Grand Prix on Crescentia!

Date: 02.0-106.00
Place: Montressor

BUSTED TODAY. The cops finally caught me.

They brought me to the inn and told my mom that next time I was going to juvenile hall. Boy, was she mad! I got the whole throwing-away-your-entire-future speech.

UGH!

So I left and went down to the docks. And that's when things really started happening!

Out of nowhere, this rickety cruiser flew overhead and crash-landed on the dock. I ran down and pulled this old spacer turtle guy out of the wreck. He was totally messed up. The guy's name was Billy Bones, and he was FREAKED OUT!!! And so was I!

He grabbed my collar and begged me to hide him. He was badly hurt. I wasn't sure what to do, so I dragged him back to Mom to see if she could help. (Man, did she love that!)

"BEWARE THE CYBORG!"

That's the last thing old Bones said right before he died and a band of pirates attacked the inn. I pocketed a golden sphere he had given me. Then Mom, our friend Dr. Doppler, and I escaped by jumping out the window—right before the pirates burned the Benbow to the ground!

We raced to Doppler's house. Finally safe, we took a look at the sphere. It had all these markings on it in a language we couldn't read. I kept playing around with it till suddenly the thing just popped open with a hum. Then—wow! A glowing 3-D map filled the room. We could see the Magellanic Cloud, the Coral Galaxy, the Cygnus Cross, the Calyan Abyss, and—I couldn't believe it—

TREASURE PLANET!

The old spacer had given me the map to Treasure Planet!

I'm going to find Treasure Planet!

Doppler was just as excited as me. He's going to pay for the whole trip.

Mom was really against it at first. She thought the situation was too dangerous. I think she was scared. Since Dad left, I'm all she really has.

But after a while she decided I could go. Doppler said it would be a good opportunity for "character building." Whatever. We're leaving for the spaceport Crescentia this morning.

I can't wait to get my hands on the treasure!

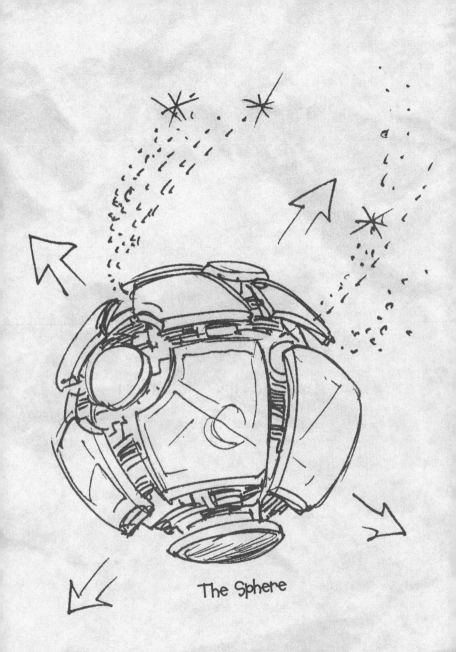

The Sphere

Things to Pack

~~Royal Galactic Passport~~   √ toothbrush and toothpaste

~~System Health Services Immunization Form~~   ~~comb~~

~~3 long-sleeved shirts~~   ~~laundry bag~~

~~2 sweaters~~   sleeping bag

~~3 pairs pants~~   ~~sheets~~

~~2 pairs shorts~~   soap

√ 5 T-shirts   ~~shampoo~~

√ 6 pairs underwear and socks   ~~flashlight~~

~~1 pair boots~~   ~~solarium crystals~~

~~1 bath towel~~   ~~water bottle~~

~~2 bandannas~~   ~~etherium sickness medication~~

Mom thinks I need all this stuff.
I think I'll pack a little lighter.

Date: 04.0–009.00
Place: Montressor

I'm having trouble sleeping tonight.

I'M JUST TOO EXCITED!

Before heading off to bed, Doppler told me he was amazed that I'd been able to open the map. "James Hawkins," he said, "during my undergraduate days I studied modern spheroid cryptology. And I didn't even come close to opening that map! Impressive, my boy, quite impressive!"

It's a shame map opening isn't a class at school. Then I would get an Ⓐ on my report card for once.

Date: 05.0–010.50
Place: Space Ferry

I'm writing this on the ferry ride to the spaceport Crescentia.

The starfields are incredible to look at. I've never left Montressor, so even this much space travel is exciting!

At the station we'll be boarding
our ship, the RLS Legacy. Doppler
hired it out for the trip.

I can't wait to see the ship. I bet it's incredible.
We're coming up to Crescentia now. There are all
these different ships and aliens I've never seen before!

Doppler has on this stupid space gear he bought from a two-headed saleswoman.

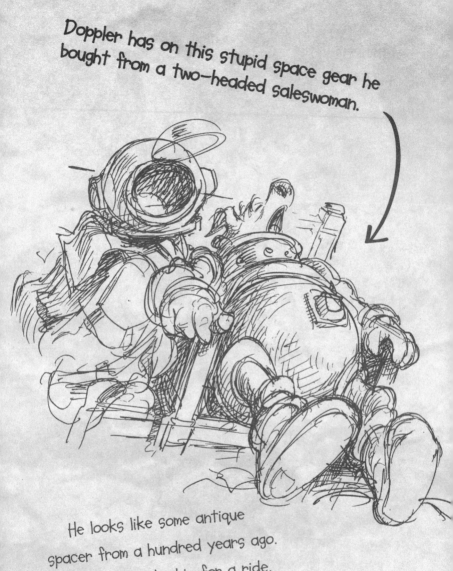

He looks like some antique
spacer from a hundred years ago.
Boy, did she take him for a ride.

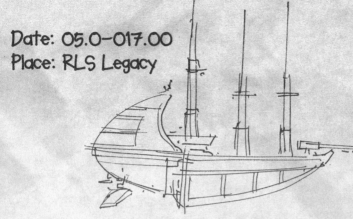

The Legacy is so cool! It's a huge solar galleon with three masts. I've never seen such an amazing ship!

After we boarded, I met the officers and some of the crew. The captain's name is Amelia. She's battled with the Procyan Armada. Tough does not even begin to describe her.

Arrow is the first mate, and he's as solid as a rock—like, for real!

The captain took our map and locked it away in a gun case in her cabin. She says everything about Treasure Planet has to be kept **TOP SECRET**. She doesn't like the crew Dr. Doppler hired. I wonder why?

The captain assigned me to work in the galley. And here I thought I was getting away from busing tables! RIGHT.

Then I met the cook, John Silver. I almost choked when I saw he was a cyborg. Bones had warned me about a cyborg! Could Silver be part of the band of pirates who burned down the Benbow Inn? I am definitely going to keep an eye on him.

But then again, would a bloodthirsty pirate have a cute pet? Silver's got a funny shape-shifter named Morph. He's a cool little guy. He does great impressions and can change himself into spoons and stuff.

More on those two later . . .

Silver let me go up on deck for the launch. It was so amazing. A warm wind was blowing and the solar sails were glistening. Just after the artificial-gravity generator ignited, the force field washed over the deck, and wow! We were off into the etherium.

Pretty soon, I spotted a pod of Orcus galacticus off the starboard side. I'd heard about them, but I'd never seen one. They're huge!

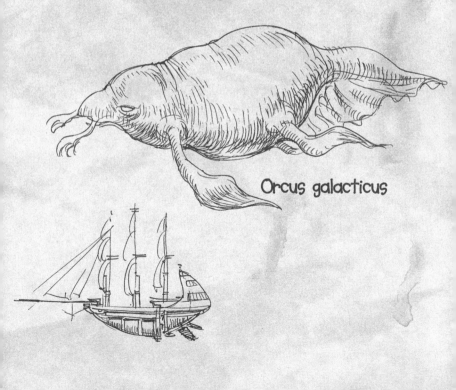

Orcus galacticus

Later on, I almost got in a fight with this jerk from the crew. They call him Scroop. He's a big ugly insectoid—looks like a spider.

I was just mopping the deck and minding my own business when the guy with two heads (or is it two guys with one head?) started with me.

Then Scroop scrambled down the rigging and joined him. I tried not to show it, but I was pretty scared. My heart was pounding and my hands were shaking. Then Silver stepped in and it was over.

Maybe I can trust that old cyborg. He DID save my life. . . .

Date: 09.0-001.00
Place: RLS Legacy

Silver told me the crew is made up of aliens from all over the galaxy! There are three main categories of crewmen—riggers, specialists, and ropers.

That guy Scroop seems to be the rigger in charge. Oxy and Moron are pretty friendly with him. The other riggers are Greedy, Dogbreath (Brush your teeth, my friend!), and Birdbrain Mary.

OXY

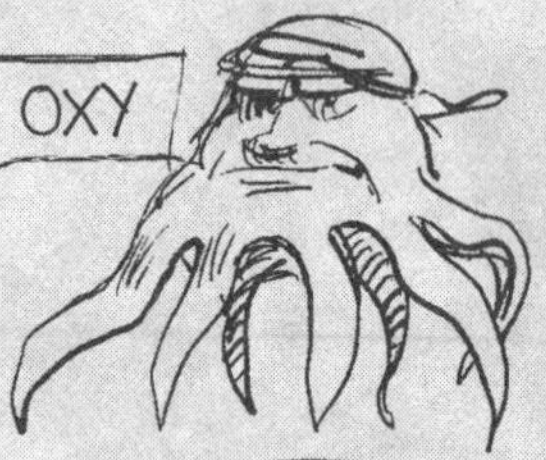

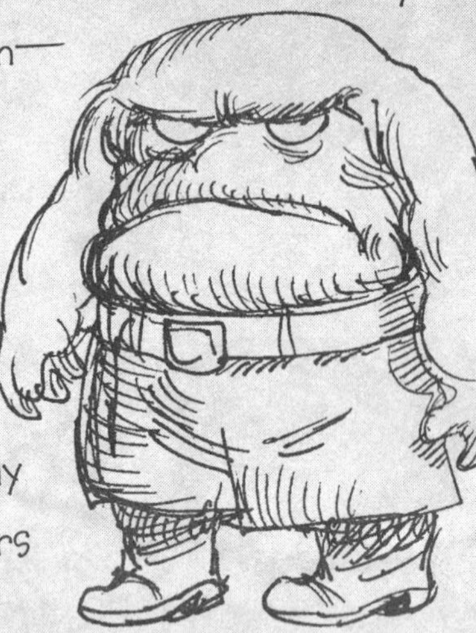

MORON

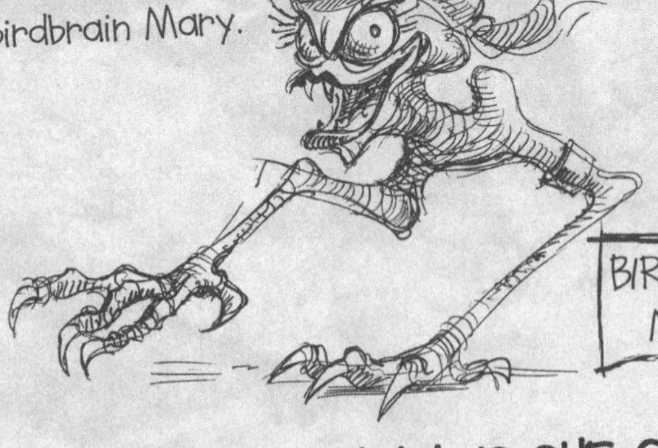

BIRDBRAIN MARY

(WOW, IS SHE CRAZY!)

Then there are the specialists.
Turnbuckle has a bunch of arms, which
are useful when you are the helmsman!

Snuff controls the antigravity device.

Onus is the lookout.

Meltdown is the mechanic.
He's also the ship's gunner.
I wonder if we'll actually
run into anything for him to
shoot at?

And then there are the
ropers: Hands, Pigors, Aquanoggin,
and Schwartzkopf. I haven't really
gotten to know any of them yet. Maybe
sometime during the trip I'll ask one of
them to show me the ropes (ha!). I've
always wanted to learn proper rigging.

TURNBUCKLE

MACKRIKI

Date: 10.0–023.50 Place:
RLS Legacy

The etherium has been a little rough during the past few hours. Too bad I tossed out the etherium sickness medicine Mom packed for me—maybe one day I'll learn.

I've had a little free time today to explore the ship. It's really just like the ships I heard about as a kid.

The Legacy is so HUGE, I don't think any cosmic storm could damage it. According to Arrow, it's made of some of the finest material in the galaxy. The masts are constructed of pure quarkwood, and the rigging is made of shining allstonium.

And in case we run into pirates, the Legacy is armed with sharpshooting laser cannons. Word has it that Meltdown is one of the finest shots in the galaxy. Those pirates had better watch out!

You hear a lot of rumors down on Montressor about pirates hiding behind every asteroid out here in the etherium.

I'll keep my eyes PEELED....

Silver said he's not going to let me out of his sight. That he's going to take me under his wing.

Whatever.

I've gotten along fine for over fifteen years. I definitely don't need a clunky old cyborg on my back.

Date: 12.0–001.00
Place: RLS Legacy

That cyborg is really working me to the bone!

Captain Amelia runs a tight ship. I think she's a really good captain.

Doppler told me that she almost single-handedly saved seven ships during a space battle, and she was the youngest spacer ever to be made a captain. She was awarded the Green Badge of Honor during the Kattindog Quasar War fifteen years ago.

That's some honor!

Date: 12.0–012.50
Place: RLS Legacy

I think we're making good time on the voyage. I wonder how close we are to Treasure Planet?

Of course, I can't ask Amelia. The rule is not to mention a single word about the real reason we are on this voyage! She's the captain. What she says goes.

Date: 12.0-031.00
Place: RLS Legacy

Man! Silver really meant it when he said he'd be keeping his eye on me. I've been working in the galley for him nonstop. If I had wanted to work this hard, I could have stayed at home with Mom!

There are a lot of mouths to feed on the Legacy! And these spacers really work up an appetite.

It can be pretty boring down in the galley. So Silver tells a lot of jokes—bad ones.

Q: How much did the pirate pay for his piercings?
A: A buck an ear!

Or—

Q: What is a pirate's favorite class in school?
A: ARRRRRRRRRRrithmetic!

At least the old cyborg makes me laugh. Morph is funny, too. His imitations are great!

My Duties

- Scrub astrobarnacles from keel

- Swab upper and lower decks

- Organize food in pantry

- Clean crow's nest

- Clean heads
  (that's spacer talk for bathrooms)

- Clean oven

- Help prepare breakfast, lunch, and dinner

- Refill all water jugs and containers

- Check all ropes and lines

*Make one café lattoid for Captain Amelia each morning, deliver at 7 A.M. sharp!

Bonzabeast Stew

You will need

1 quart bonzabeast broth	5 purps, seeded and pureed
1 bonzabeast, defuzzed	16 planktonics from the Calyan Abyss, coarsely chopped

- Bring bonzabeast broth to a low simmer. Remember to plug your nose, since boiling bonzabeast can raise a stench that will hoist the sails on your solar galleon.
- Wash bonzabeast meat and pat dry. Be sure that all traces of fur have been removed or your guests will develop hairballs of galactic proportions.
- Add bonzabeast meat to broth, stirring slowly. (Be sure to include all 12 eyeballs for added flavor.)
- Add purp juice and chopped planktonics, whisking thoroughly. Allow to simmer over low flame for 11 1/2 Procyan hours.
- Ladle into bowls and serve immediately.

Enjoy!

Morph scammed some of my stew disguised as a spoon!

Date: 12.0–066.00
Place: RLS Legacy

I did the dinner dishes quickly tonight and had some free time. Silver said he had something to show me. We went up on deck just as we were sailing past Saxonite. I would love to surf the rings around that planet!

Up in the crow's nest, Silver showed me how to tie a bunch of different knots. The first knot was really tough, but I finally got it with a little practice. Then Silver taught me some more, like the Black Hole Bowline, the Andromeda Square, and the Quasar Clove Hitch.

Silver said soon enough, I'll be able to rig a sail mast.

Cool!

HOW TO TIE KNOTS

Quasar Clove Hitch

This knot is easy to tie and untie. It is often used to tie a boat to a post.

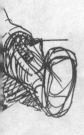

1. Wrap the free end of the rope around a post. Bring it across the longer end.

2. Run the free end around the post again in the same direction as before. Make sure the place where the rope crosses is loose. The two loops should not cross each other.

3. Weave the free end beneath the place where the rope crosses over itself. Pull on both ends to tighten the knot.

Andromeda Square

This is a quick knot to tie. However, it will sometimes come untied with movement. It shouldn't be used to tie two ropes together.

1. Wrap the rope around an object and tie two overhand knots. (Remember this trick: left over right and through, then right over left and through.)

2. Pull evenly on the two free ends.

Black Hole Bowline

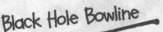

This is one of the most useful knots. It makes a strong, secure loop that is easy to tie and untie.

1. Make a loop by passing the free end (short end) of the rope over the longer end.

2. Pass the free end under and up through the loop hole. Leave a second larger loop beneath the first loop.

3. Run the free end over the longer end, then around behind it and back through the smaller loop. Hold the free end and pull lightly on the longer end to tighten the knot. Using both hands, grab the larger loop and the longer end of the rope and pull tight.

Date: 12.5-001.00
Place: RLS Legacy

The spacer I like best on this ship isn't a spacer at all. It's Morph, Silver's pet. He is so funny, always changing shapes and playing jokes.

That little squidge!

Silver's not so bad, either. He orders the crew around sometimes. But for some reason, they really listen to him.

He's always telling them stories. Sometimes I overhear the tales. Boy, Silver sure has had some dangerous adventures. And he's sailed all over the etherium, from the Andrien Asteroids to the Zanzibar Star!

At first I really didn't trust that old bag of bolts, but he's growing on me.

The rest of the crew— well, it's better than hanging out with the kids at school, I guess.

Date: 12.5-002.00
Place: RLS Legacy

The etherium sure is peaceful tonight.

I'm sitting here in the crow's nest. I can see clear across the galaxy. I wonder if we'll ever get to Treasure Planet. Even if we do, will we find Flint's trove?

Today Silver taught me an old spacer song. It goes like this:

Fifteen spacers on a dead man's chest
Yo ho ho here on Proteus One
Methinks the pirate done for the rest
Yo ho ho here on Proteus One

The mate was fixed by the robot's spark
The robot brained with a Calypsian spike
Cook's heart was marked like it
Had been gripped by alien fingers twelve
And there they all good dead spacers like
Break o' day in an asteroid den
Yo ho ho here on Proteus One

Fifteen spacers on a whole ship's list
Yo ho ho here on Proteus One
Dead and be darned and the rest gone whist
Yo ho ho here on Proteus One

 **RLS** Legacy Crew

The first mate lay with his nob in gore
Where the pirate's ax his cheek had shore
And the robot was shorted times four and
There he lay and the etherium skies
Dripped all day in three up-staring eyes at
Montressor sunset and foul surprise
Yo ho ho here on Proteus One

Fifteen spacers on a dead man's chest
Yo ho ho here on Proteus One
Methinks the pirate done for the rest
Yo ho ho here on Proteus One

Date: 13.0-059.00
Place: RLS Legacy

Last night I fell asleep washing the dishes—

HOW EMBARRASSING!

When I woke up, I realized that Silver had covered me with a warm blanket. For such a salty cyborg, I think he can be a real softy.

It seems like we've been on this ship forever! Captain Amelia is always barking orders at me. She's all right, though. Arrow has been a good first mate. He keeps things running smoothly.

I can tell Doppler is really excited about finding Treasure Planet. I can't believe he's been able to keep the secret.

Date: 13.0-060.00
Place: RLS Legacy

Today Silver and I went out in a longboat.

I'd never been on a longboat before. First Silver showed me how to use the tiller. Then he taught me how to control the speed. After a little while, he let me take over. I was totally cruising. That boat was humming like a solar surfer.

Later I even showed Silver a few of my solar surfing moves. I almost flipped over trying the Cygnus spin. I didn't do it on purpose—but it was worth it to see the crusty old cyborg's expression—I never thought I'd see him look scared.

When I get back to Montressor, people are gonna look at me differently—a LOT differently!

I don't even know where to start. For once it felt like I was doing stuff right—but then everything fell apart.

It all started when the star Pellucid went supernova! The ship was being tossed around like a toy.

The captain ordered me to tie down the lifelines. So I did. **I SWEAR I DID.** I know those knots. I practice all the time!

I can't believe I missed that ONE knot! Did I miss it? I swear, I checked them all!

Arrow is gone. He got sucked into the black hole.

And it is ALL MY FAULT.

Date: 14.0-040.00
Place: RLS Legacy

Don't feel like writing much. I still can't believe what I did. I keep going over and over it in my mind. And every time, I remember securing his lifeline.

Silver just came up on deck and gave me a big pep talk. He told me that what happened to Arrow wasn't my fault.

I didn't believe him at first. But then I started to believe that this half-mechanical guy might be right. He said I have "THE MAKIN'S OF GREATNESS" in me. Maybe he's just trying to make me feel better. But you know, I think maybe I could be great.

Silver said I've got to chart my own course. But how can I do that when I FEEL SO TOTALLY LOST?!

Maybe he's right. Maybe I do have the makings of greatness.

I JUST HOPE I GET A CHANCE TO PROVE IT SOON.

Mr. Arrow

A finer spacer than most of us
could ever hope to be.

Date: 14.0—054.00
Place: RLS Legacy

Every time we sail past a new planet, I wonder if my dad might be there. Working at some mining job, maybe.

Sometimes I wish he'd come back home. But it's been so many years now, I don't think that's going to happen.

Silver's calling—

BACK TO THOSE CHORES...

Date: 16.0–022.00
Place: Treasure Planet

SILVER IS A PIRATE!

Luckily I keep this journal in my pocket, or else I would have lost it. I've got a second to scribble in it right now.

That lying traitor and the rest of the crew mutinied today. I can't believe it! It all happened so fast. I was in the kitchen when I overheard them planning to capture us. Then I scrambled out of my hiding place to warn the captain, but found myself face to face with that scurvy space dog Silver. All along he's been pretending to be my friend. And all he really wanted was to get to the treasure. So I jammed a pick in his cyborg leg and ran up on deck. I was so ready to get Amelia and bust him. But it was too late! The pirates had raised their flag. The takeover had already started!

We barely escaped in a longboat. And then the pirates blasted us with a laser cannon and we crash-landed on Treasure Planet. I'm here with Amelia, Doppler, and Morph.

We're in the jungle somewhere. And the whole time I thought I still had the map—it was just Morph! The real map is still on the Legacy. I was so mad at Morph. I wanted to send him straight back to Proteus One!

As if all this weren't bad enough, this crazy robot named B.E.N. found us. He keeps babbling about his missing memory chip and Captain Flint's hidden treasure. And for some reason, he always wants to hug me.

Amelia is resting and Doppler is taking care of her. She got hurt in the crash. As soon as she's ready, we're going to B.E.N.'s place so we can figure out what we're going to do next.

Amelia, Doppler, B.E.N., and I had been hiding out in B.E.N.'s house. When we heard gunfire, we knew the pirates had found us!

Silver called for a truce. I could barely stand seeing his cyborg face and his ugly fake smile.

When I saw Silver waving a white flag, I knew exactly what he wanted—

THE MAP!

That's good news—Silver and the pirates think I actually have the map. Little do they know, it's really back on the ship!

So I went out to meet Silver. I was exactly right. He wanted to bargain for the map.

Silver was trying to play it cool, as if he had never told the crew in the galley that he cared more about the treasure than anything else. He offered me half the treasure if I gave him the map.

YEAH, RIGHT.

Like I'd believe anything that guy has to say. I'm way smarter than he realizes.

Even if I did have the map, I would never hand it over to him.

If there's one thing that traitor taught me, it's to stick to my guns and not back down. And that's what I'm gonna do. Find Flint's treasure on my own—without Silver.

And boy, was he steaming mad! He shouted,
"EITHER I GET THAT MAP BY DAWN TOMORROW,
OR SO HELP ME, I'LL USE THE SHIP'S CANNONS TO
BLAST YOU ALL TO KINGDOM COME!" And then he
stomped away.

Morph was so scared, he stayed with me. I guess
he's had to learn a few things the hard way, too.

The real Silver!

Date: 20.0—009.00
Place: Treasure Planet

I'm heading back to the Legacy to get the map.

I think that weirdo robot B.E.N. may be able to help me. If he doesn't get me killed first! He can't remember anything because of that lost memory chip.

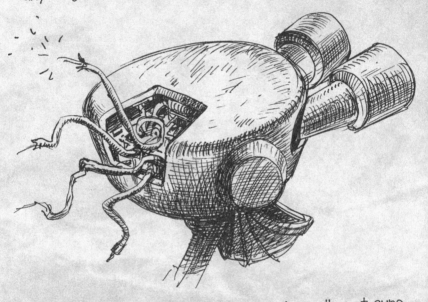

How he ended up on this planet I'm really not sure. But he does at least have some basic knowledge of how to get around. Without his help, we would have been finished a long time ago.

We're running out of time. The pirates are closing in. I've got to get my act together and do something— right now! If I don't write again, it's because things went wrong. REALLY WRONG.

I haven't had any time to write during all the craziness . . . but we're finally back and things are cool again.

MAN, AM I GLAD THAT WILD RIDE IS FINALLY OVER.

B.E.N., Morph, and I stole a longboat and sneaked back to the Legacy to find the map. And guess who tried to stop us—Scroop! He'd been left behind to guard the ship. I thought I was a goner, but then B.E.N. disabled the ship's gravity field and Scroop and I floated up above the deck. I managed to grab on to the mast and Scroop held on to the pirate flag. All of a sudden, the flag's rope broke free. Scroop hurtled into the etherium.

HE WAS HISTORY!

When we got back to B.E.N.'s house, we discovered that Silver and the rest of the pirates had captured Amelia and Doppler.

I was forced to give Silver the map. But he couldn't open it, so he demanded that I do it.

I had no choice—Doppler and Amelia were in danger! So I opened the map. This incredible corkscrewing path appeared, going out the window and over the horizon. I gave the pirates a taste, and then I closed the map. I told Silver, "If you want the map, you're takin' me, too."

You should've seen the look on his face as he realized he'd have to give in. We would all venture to find Flint's treasure . . . together.

So we got in the pirates' longboat and followed the path. After sailing through the jungle, we arrived at a sheer cliff.

Once again, nobody could figure out what to do. Of course those idiot pirates were ready to kill me. **DUH**—like that was going to help them find the treasure. Then one of the pirates knocked me to the ground and that's when I saw it—ancient writings on the ground that matched the ones on the map. I placed the map on top of the pattern.

Suddenly there was this huge triangle—like a door to anywhere in the universe. From where we were standing, we could easily see the Lagoon Nebula, which is on the other side of the galaxy!

So _this_ was how Flint had roamed the universe, robbing ships in every corner of every galaxy. By using the portal, he and his band of brigands could strike anywhere they wanted. And then, with just the push of a button, they'd return to Treasure Planet to hide their booty.

BUT WHERE WAS FLINT'S TREASURE?

Then I remembered—B.E.N. had been babbling earlier about "the centroid of the mechanism." I thought he was talking nonsense. But he really was telling me where Flint's trove was!

I hit an image in the middle of the map and there it was . . . treasure from all over the universe. Mountains of it! JEWELS. GOLD. DRUBLOONS. PAINTINGS. GEMS. CROWNS. GOBLETS. STATUES. And on top of this pile of treasure, Flint's ship—with more booty inside! The pirates didn't care about me now. This was my chance to escape! I decided to take Flint's ship. I'd get away from the pirates with plenty of loot!

But Flint had made sure that nobody would ever get his treasure. I found B.E.N.'s missing memory chip in the hand of the ancient pirate's skeleton. I put it back into the empty slot in B.E.N.'s head. That's when B.E.N. started remembering. The place was booby-trapped! The entire center of the planet started to self-destruct. Everyone freaked. The whole place was shaking and exploding. Huge crevasses opened up, and the treasure started falling into them. In a couple minutes, we were all gonna be history! I started up old Flint's ship. But Silver had the same idea. He climbed on board and started toward me. . . . Suddenly the ship lurched, and we both fell over the rail. The ship was being sucked into an energy beam!

You're never going to believe what happened next. I was barely hanging on, about to fall to my death. Silver was struggling to hold on to the ship and pull it out of the energy beam. He had to make a choice: save me, or save his lifelong dream——the treasure.

Luckily for me, he let go of the ship and pulled me to safety.

Silver and I escaped through the portal, but we weren't safe yet.

THE WHOLE PLANET WAS FALLING APART!

Luckily, Doppler and Amelia had captured the pirates and taken control of the longboat. They flew to the Legacy and steered the ship to the triangular portal just in time for Silver and me to jump aboard.

KA-BOOM!!!!!!!

Debris smashed into the ship and broke the sails. The Legacy was too damaged to make the escape. The clock was ticking! I knew then that the only way to escape was through the portal. I needed Silver's help. We got together a bunch of metal and spare parts from the ship's cannons. Silver did what I told him and started welding. (That cyborg arm of his came in handy!) In just a few minutes, we built a makeshift surfer! It wasn't much, but it was just what we needed.

I kicked the cylinder into gear and shot toward the portal. I had to dodge all these flying hunks of machinery! I flew through a hole in one of them, crouching and spinning upside down. Before I knew it, I was flying over the map controller. As I sailed past, still upside down, I reached out and hit the right button.

As I flew through the portal, everyone on the ship's deck cheered. Crescentia glowed in the distance. And just past that ... Montressor! I never thought I'd be so glad to see that planet. **HOME**. We'd done it!

I made a pinpoint landing on the deck of the ship. Morph flew up and licked me! B.E.N. gave me a great big robot hug. Amelia and Doppler were really proud.

But where was Silver?

I went down to the hangar bay looking for him. And there I caught him . . . . about to get into a longboat. He was trying to escape, of course. The punishment for mutiny is severe. I don't think Silver really wanted to face the judge and spend the rest of his life in jail—or worse!

Silver asked me to ship out with him. "Hawkins and Silver!" he said. "Out on our own!" I thought about it for a second. But if there's one thing I learned from that bucket of bolts, it's that I have to chart my own course.

We hugged each other goodbye. We both had tears in our eyes.

He gave me a handful of jewels to help rebuild the Benbow Inn. Then he was off through the doors of the hangar bay, his laughter echoing in my ears.

I'm really going to miss that old cyborg. But at least I still have Morph—Silver left the little squidge with me.

Date: 29.0–028.50
Place: Crescentia

We're unloading at the dock on Crescentia right now. Getting ready to return to Montressor. Here come the robot cops to take away the mutineers. For once, they're not after me!

Amelia just gave me great news. She'll be writing me a letter of recommendation to the Astro Academy. She said they could use a man like me. Just wait until Mom hears that. She'll be <u>so</u> proud of me!

Mom was so happy to see me in one piece!

We had a big dinner together at Doppler's house. We told Mom all about our adventure—the voyage, the pirates, and Treasure Planet itself. Well, Doppler and I did leave out the most dangerous parts. We didn't want Mom to worry too much.

After dinner we went to see Amelia in the hospital. She's recovering well from her injuries and should be home tomorrow. I'm sure that soon enough, she'll be off on her next voyage.

Mom is so excited that we're going to rebuild the Benbow. Without the jewels Silver gave me, it wouldn't be possible. It's going to be a lot of work, but it'll be even **bigger** and **better** than before.

BEFORE

AFTER

Date: 29.0–064.00
Place: Montressor

Wow. I sure have written a lot. I'll have to start a new journal when I enter the academy. (I'm keeping my fingers crossed.)

I guess a lot has happened!

I've been thinking lately about Silver and everything he taught me.

You know what? Before I left Montressor, I was still a boy. Nobody took me seriously. But things are different now. Silver told me I've got "the makin's of greatness" in me. And I finally believe him.

It never would have happened if it weren't for that old pirate who helped me find the real treasure—the one inside myself!

To: Admiral Bruce T. Bluedwarf III, Royal Galactic Navy

Re: Recommendation for James P. Hawkins for entrance into the RGAA

Dear Admiral Bluedwarf:

It is with distinct pleasure that I recommend Mr. James Pleiades Hawkins for entrance into the Royal Galactic Astro Academy.

On my most recent voyage, Mr. Hawkins initially came aboard as a cabin boy. During his tenure in stated position, he performed his chores dutifully and admirably.

Unfortunately, severe problems surfaced. The crew turned out to be nothing more than a group of snarling pirates. A vicious mutiny ensued.

During the struggle against the pirates, Mr. Hawkins acted with the utmost bravery and intelligence. He battled with skill and determination, despite the fact that we were greatly outnumbered by our foes.

Moreover, Mr. Hawkins's quick thinking, resourcefulness, and natural gifts as a sailor saved the day. His piloting of a solar surfer built on the spot demonstrated not only very impressive engineering skills, but also an astounding aptitude for all things nautical.

Never in my long and distinguished career have I encountered a youth with such potential and character. Jim will surely make an outstanding addition to the student body at the academy, and will without a doubt be a fine captain in the future.

Please contact me if you have any questions.

Sincerely,

Captain Amelia

Captain Amelia
RGAA Class of 005